LITTLE MOUSE
Gets Ready

JEFF SMITH

Little Mouse

Gets Ready

A TOON BOOK BY

JEFF SMITH

TOON BOOKS IS A DIVISION OF **RAW** JUNIOR, LLC, NEW YORK

A THEODOR SEUSS GEISEL HONOR BOOK
A SCHOOL LIBRARY JOURNAL BEST COMICS FOR KIDS 2009 SELECTION
A JUNIOR LIBRARY GUILD SELECTION

For Kathleen Glosan

Editorial Director: FRANÇOISE MOULY

Book Design: JONATHAN BENNETT & FRANÇOISE MOULY

Colors: STEVE HAMAKER

JEFF SMITH'S artwork was drawn with ink on paper and digitally colored.

Copyright © 2009 Jeff Smith. A TOON Book, published by RAW Junior, LLC, 27 Greene Street, New York, NY 10013. Printed in Singapore by Tien Wah Press (Pte.) Ltd. No part of this book may be used or reproduced in any manner whatsoever without written permission except in the case of brief quotations embodied in critical articles and reviews. All rights reserved. TOON Books, LITTLE LIT® and THE LITTLE LIT LIBRARY are trademarks of RAW Junior, LLC.

Library of Congress Cataloging-in-Publication Data:

Smith, Jeff, 1960 Feb. 27-

Little Mouse gets ready / by Jeff Smith.

p. cm.   "A Toon Book."   Summary: Little Mouse gets dressed to go to the barn with his mother, brothers, and sisters.

ISBN 978-1-935179-01-6

1. Graphic novels. [1. Graphic novels. 2. Mice—Fiction. 3. Clothing and dress—Fiction.] I. Title.

PZ7.7.S64Li 2009   741.5'973--dc22   2008055403

ISBN 13: 978-1-935179-01-6   ISBN 10: 1-935179-01-2

10 9 8 7 6 5 4 3 2

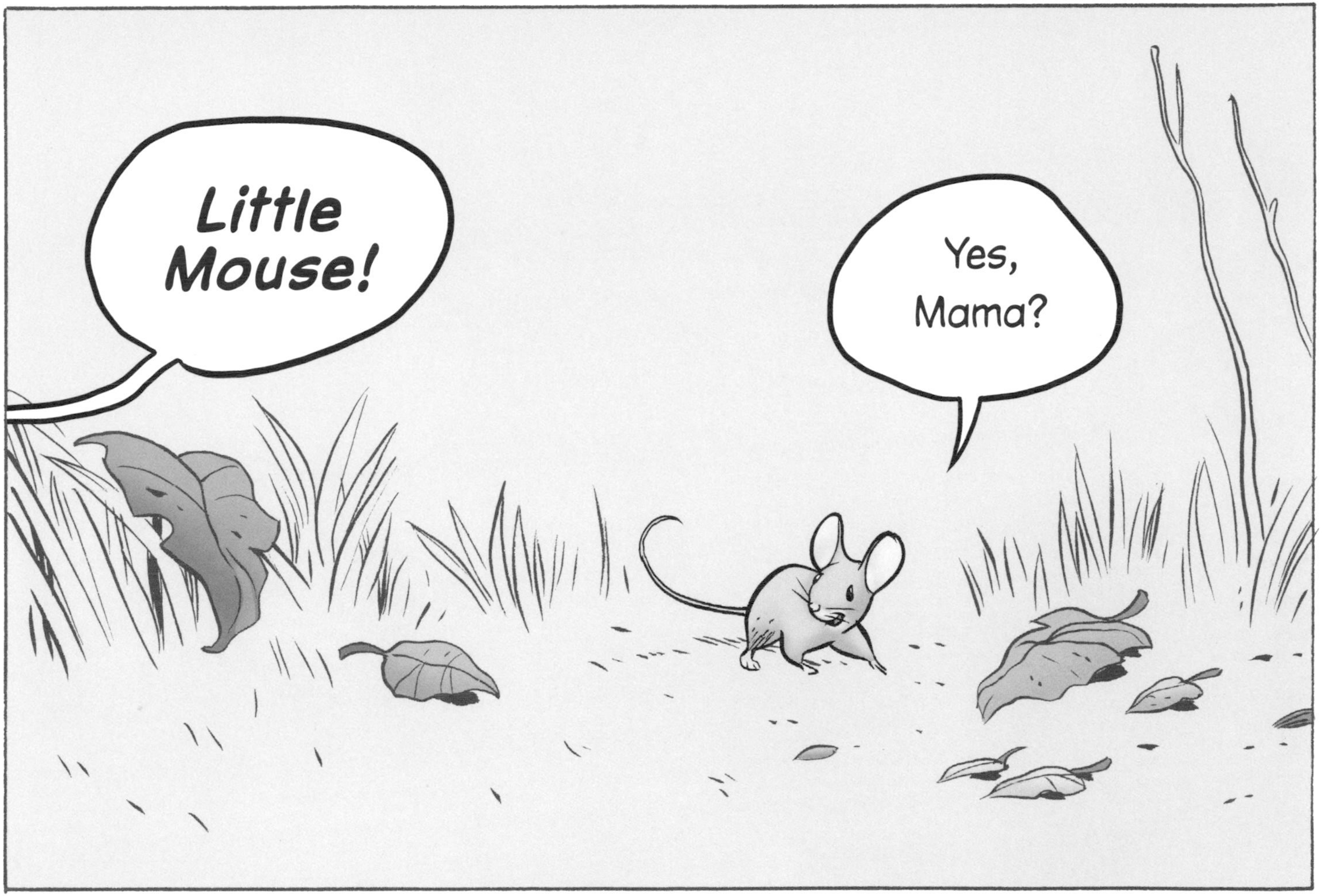
Little Mouse!
Yes, Mama?

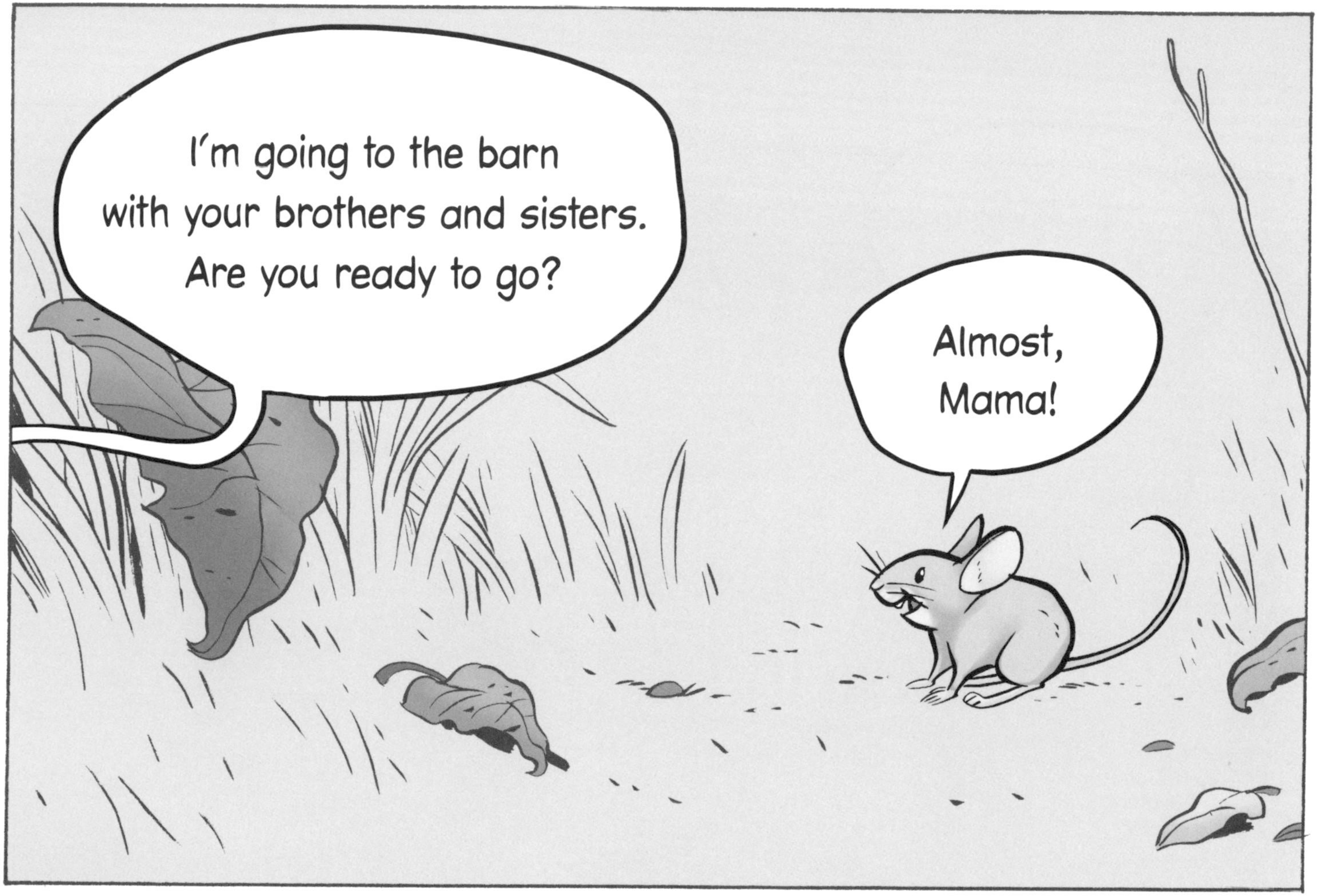
I'm going to the barn with your brothers and sisters. Are you ready to go?
Almost, Mama!

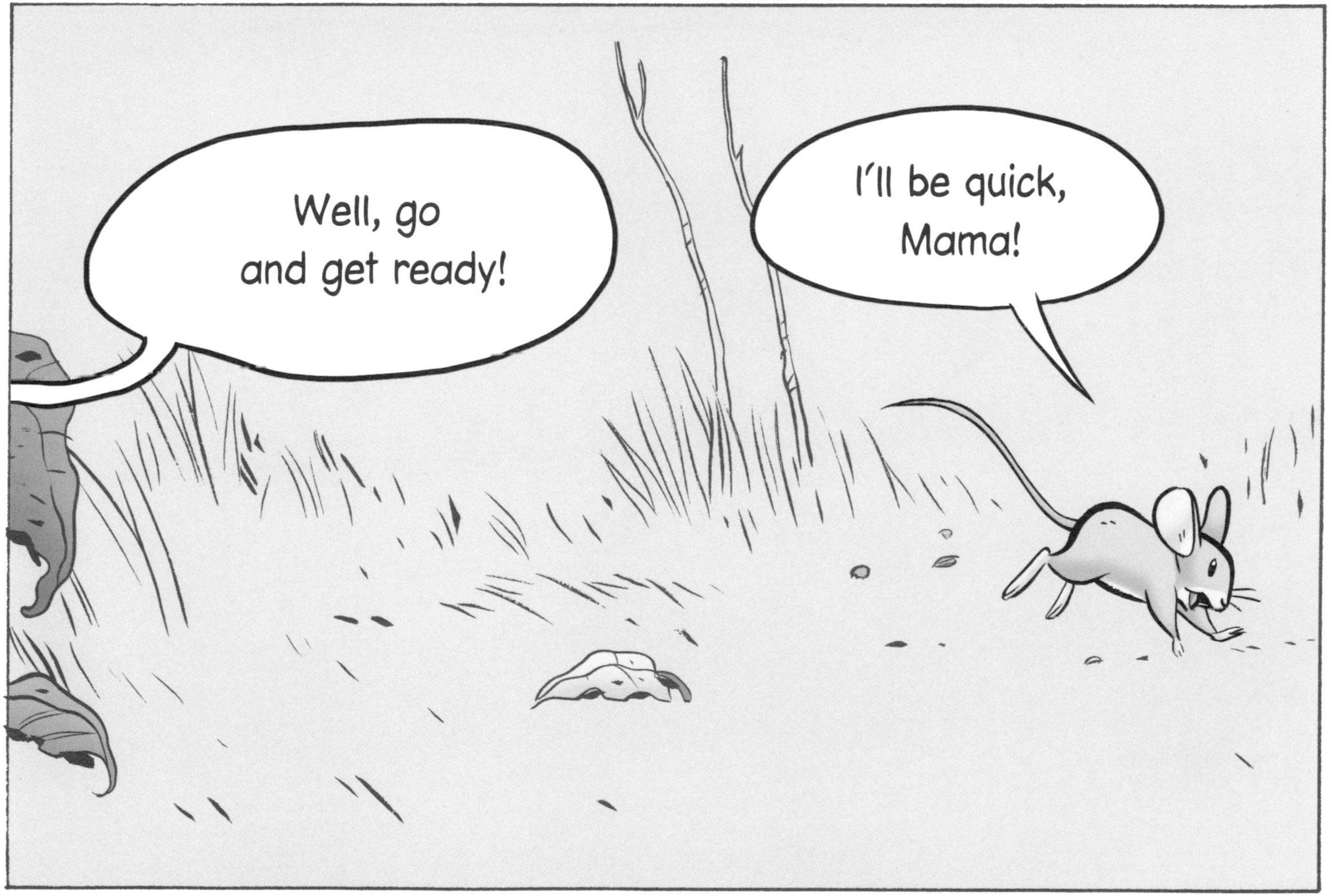
Well, go and get ready!
I'll be quick, Mama!

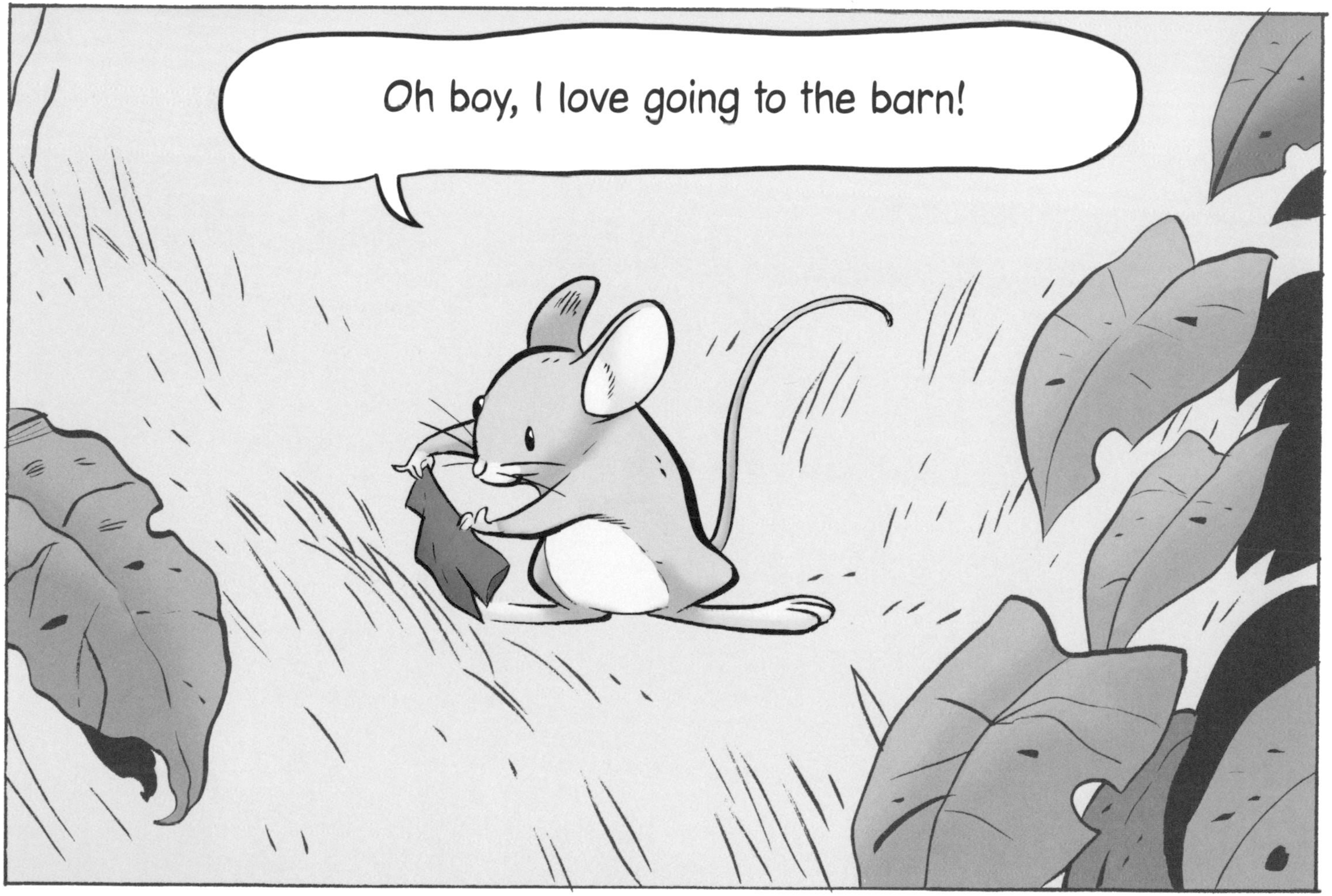
Oh boy, I love going to the barn!

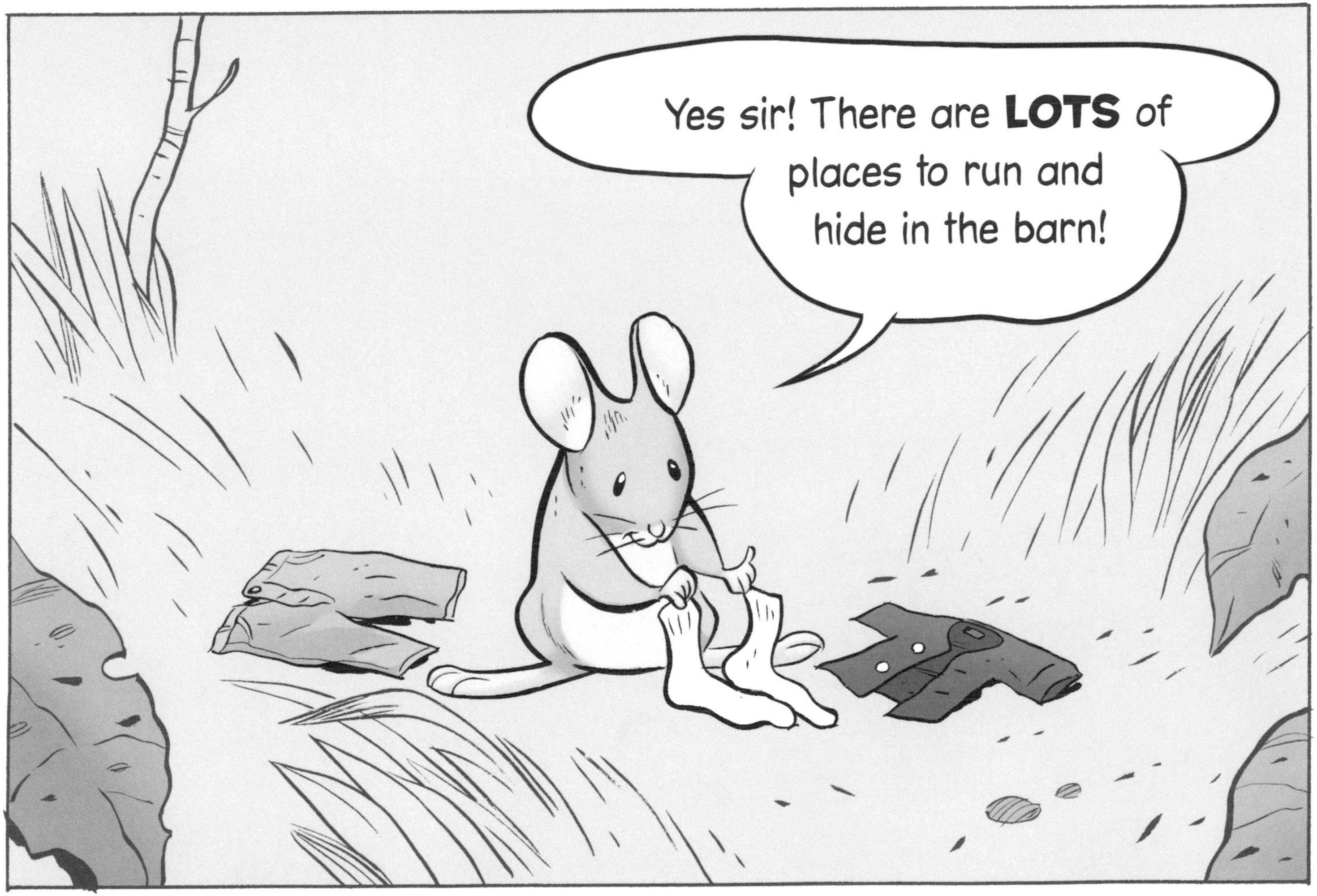
Yes sir! There are **LOTS** of places to run and hide in the barn!

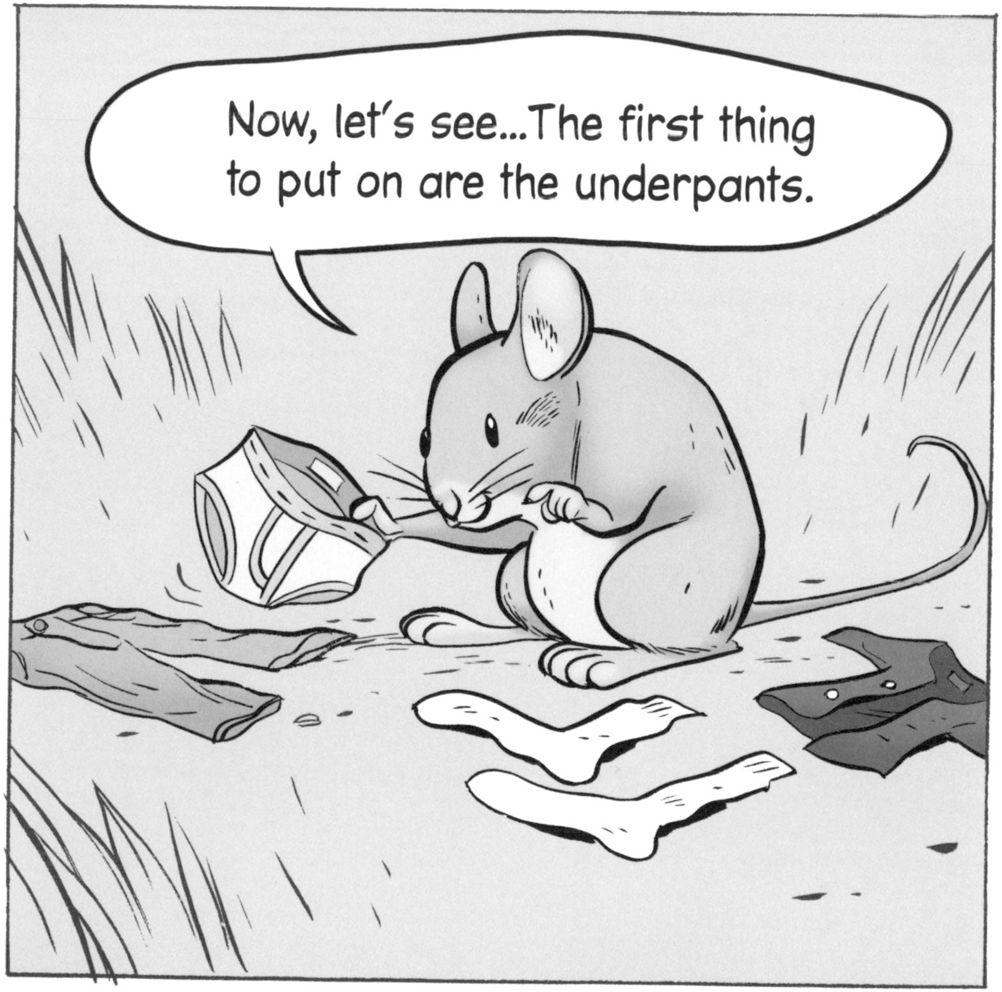
Now, let's see...The first thing to put on are the underpants.

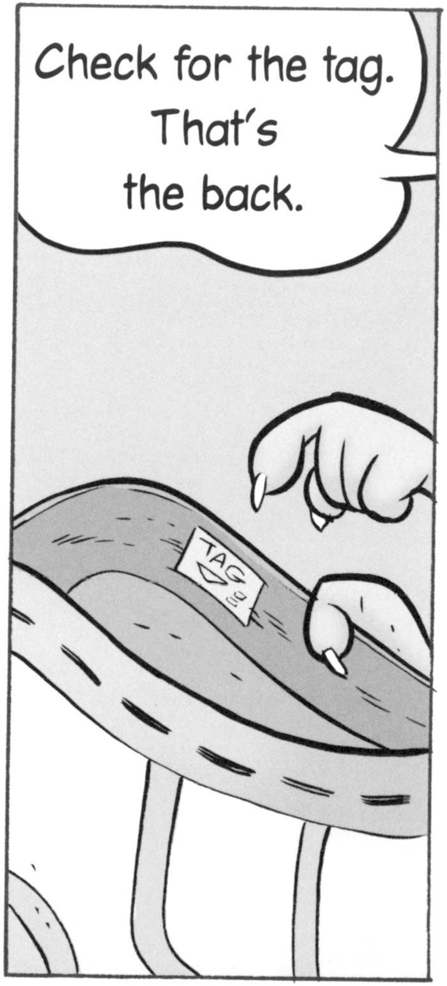
Check for the tag. That's the back.
TAG

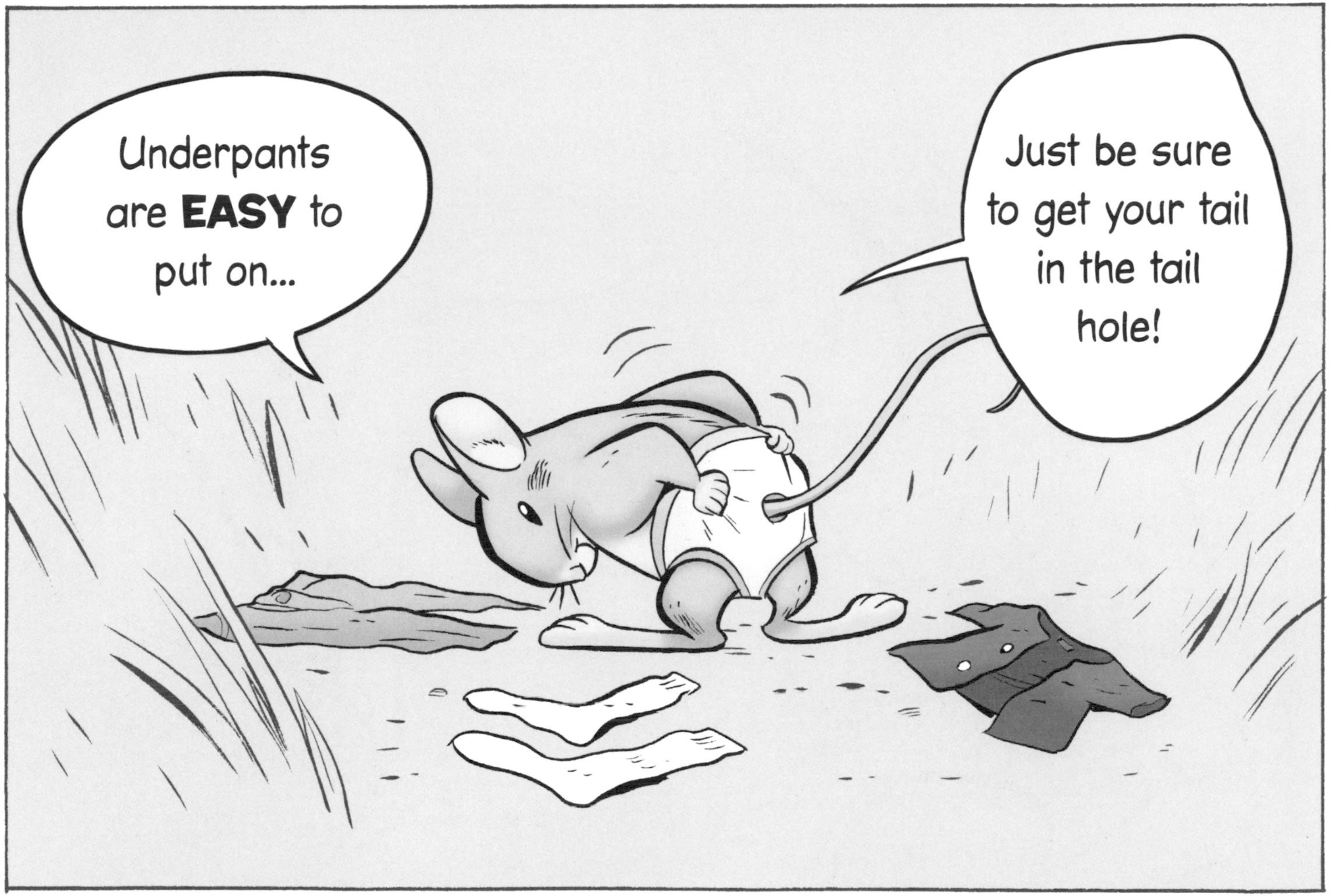
Underpants are **EASY** to put on...
Just be sure to get your tail in the tail hole!

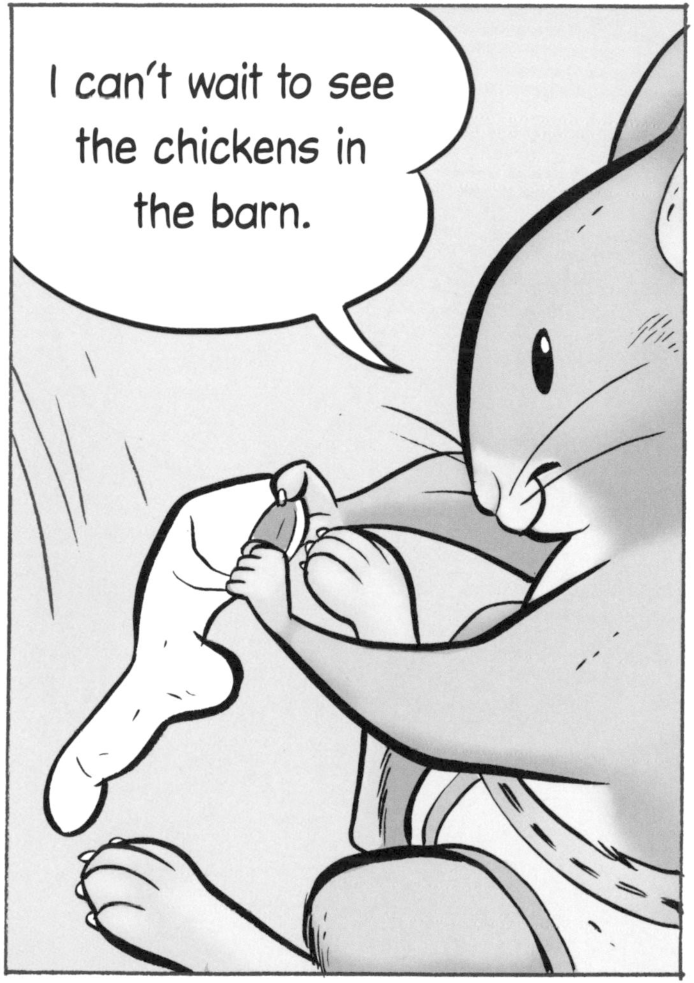
I can't wait to see the chickens in the barn.

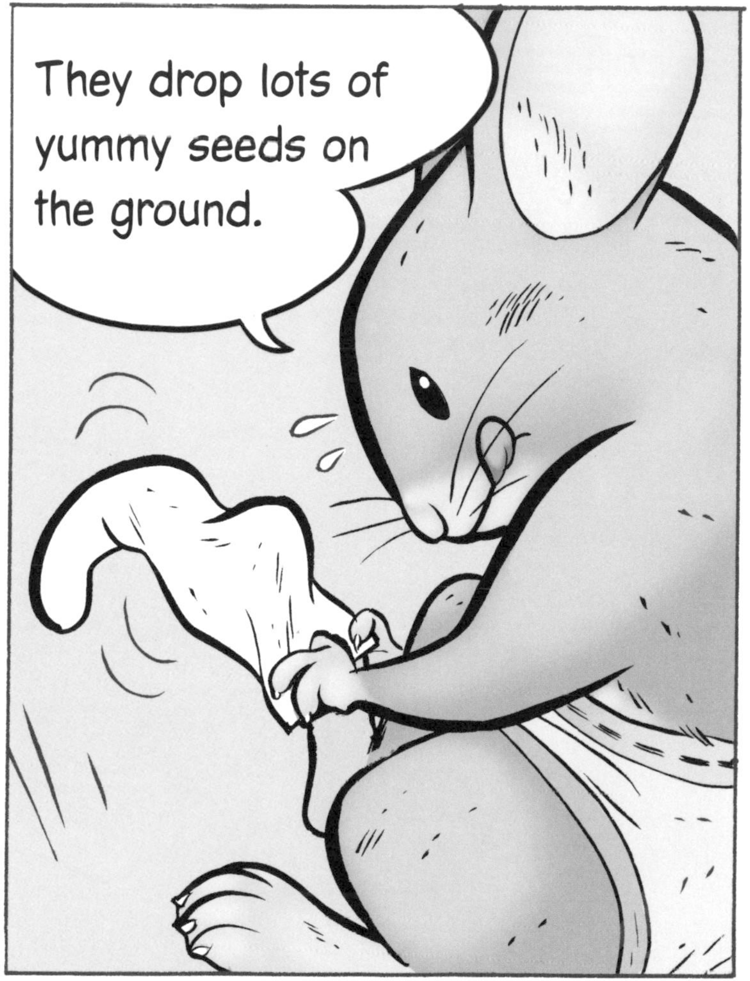
They drop lots of yummy seeds on the ground.

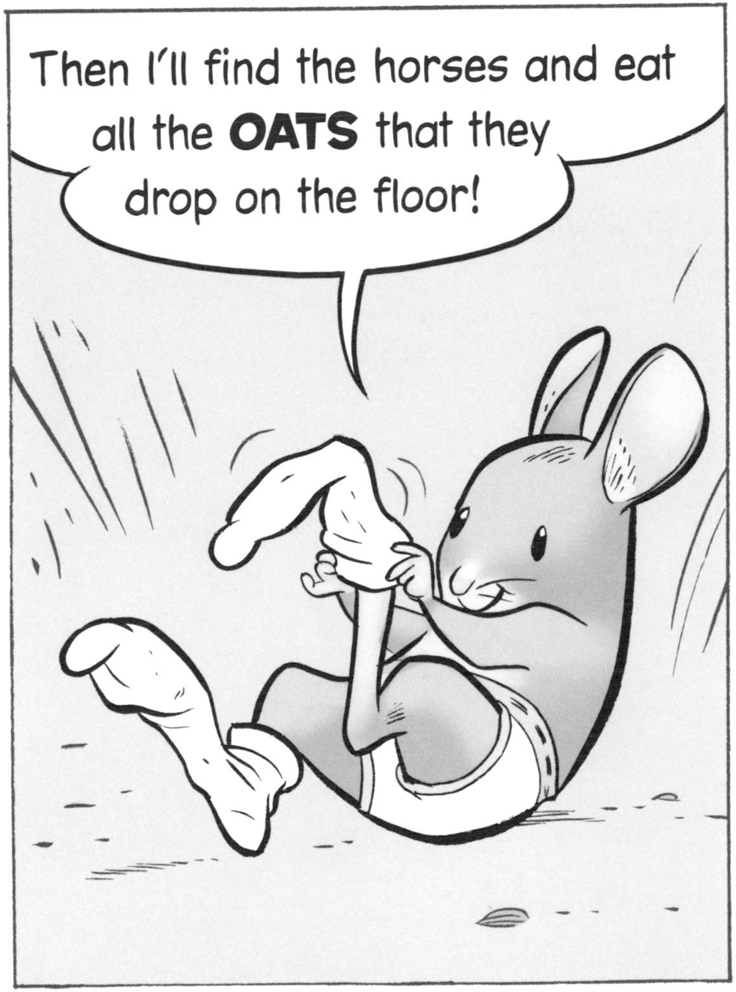
Then I'll find the horses and eat all the **OATS** that they drop on the floor!

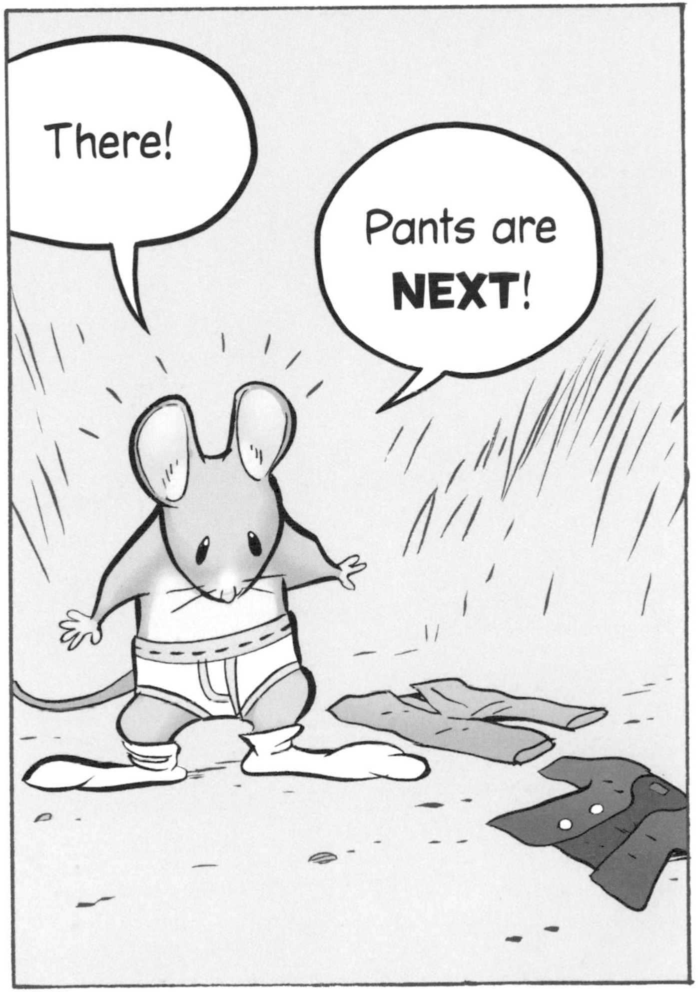
There!
Pants are **NEXT**!

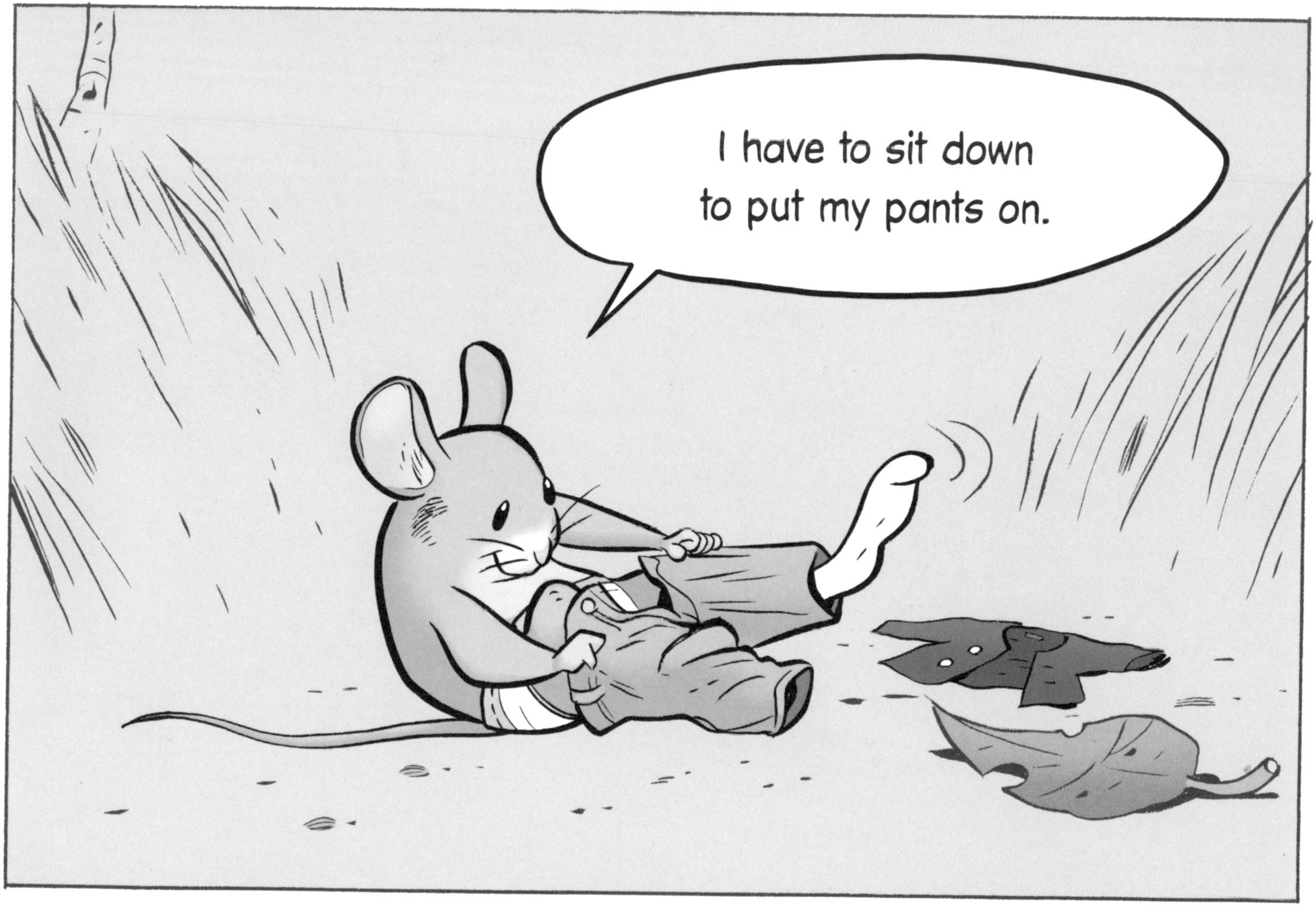
I have to sit down
to put my pants on.

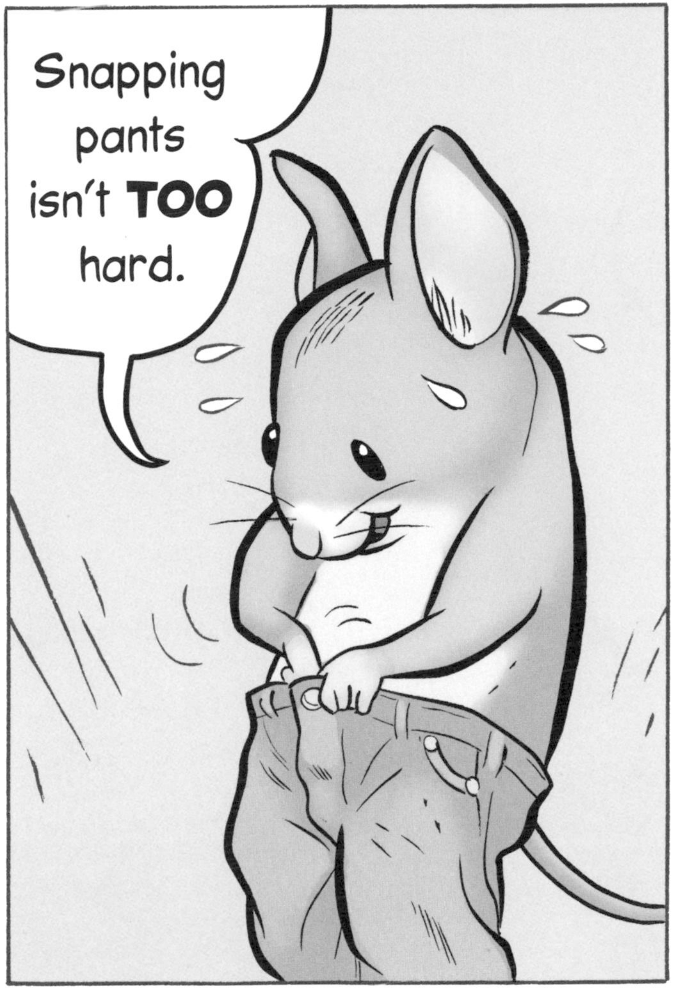
Snapping pants isn't **TOO** hard.

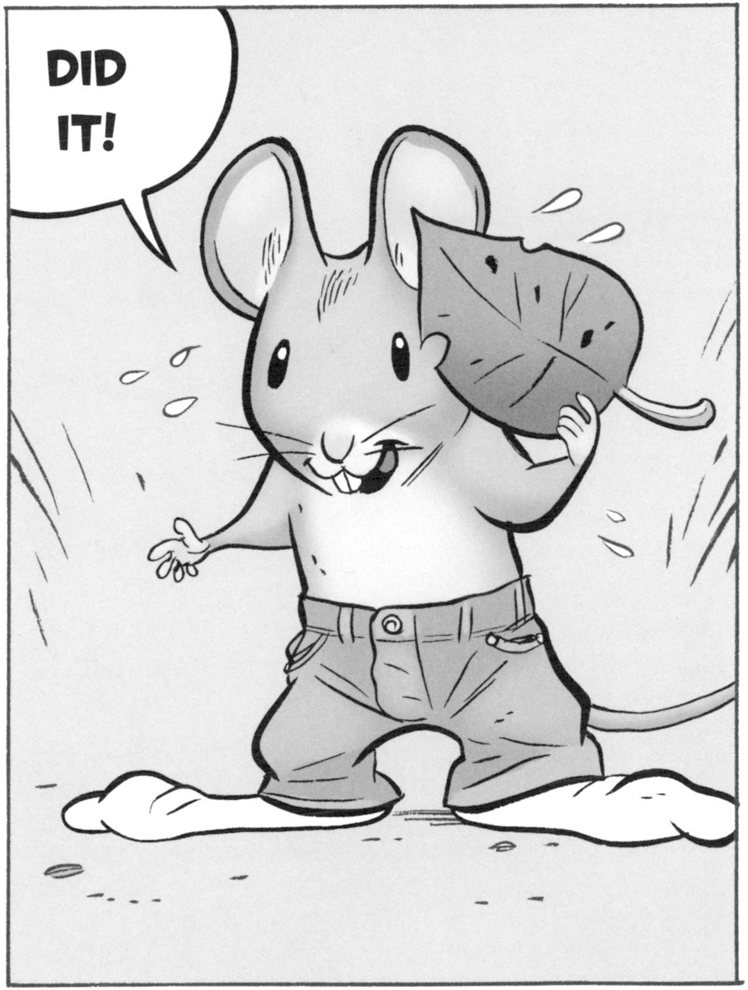
DID IT!

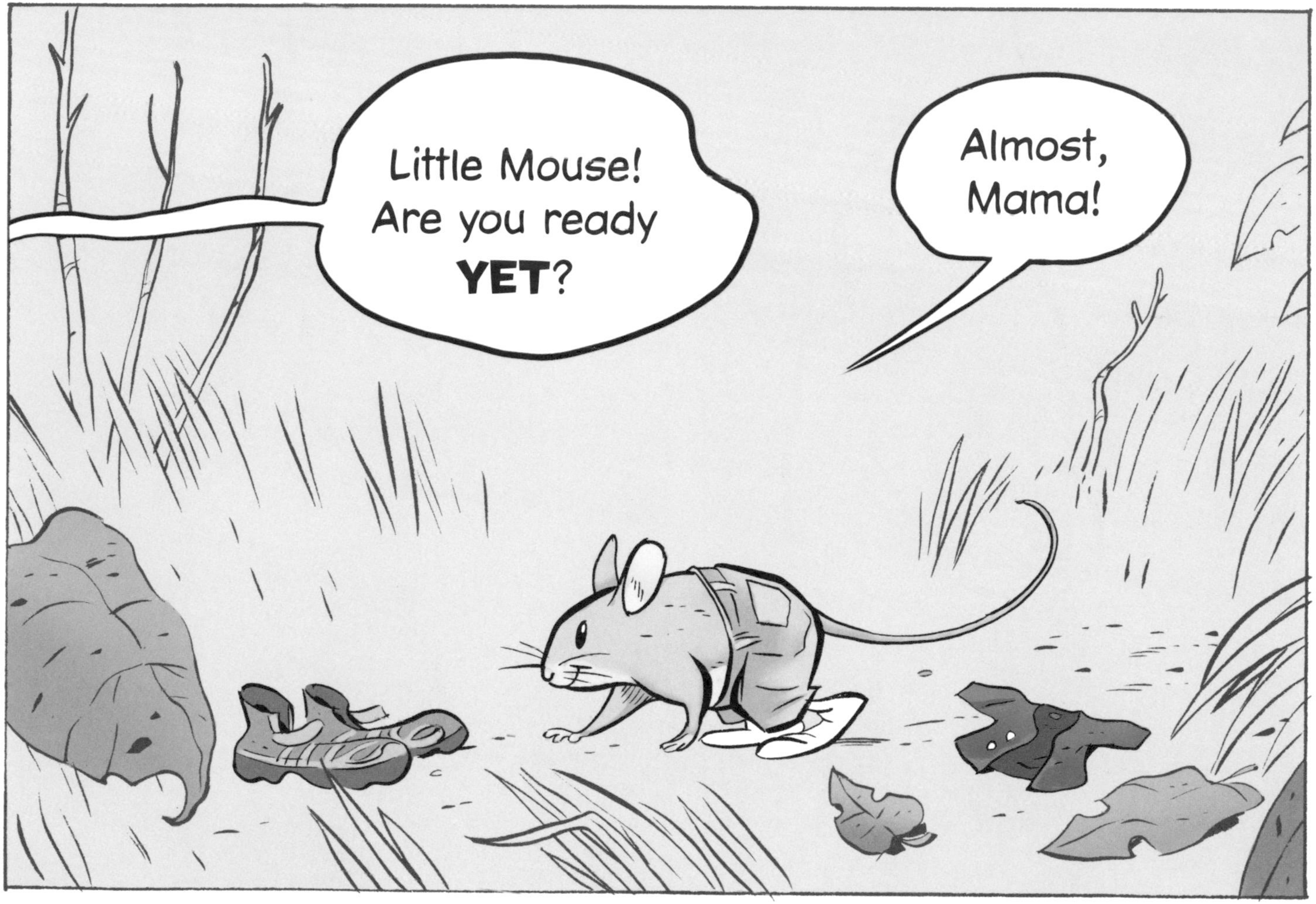
Little Mouse! Are you ready **YET**?
Almost, Mama!

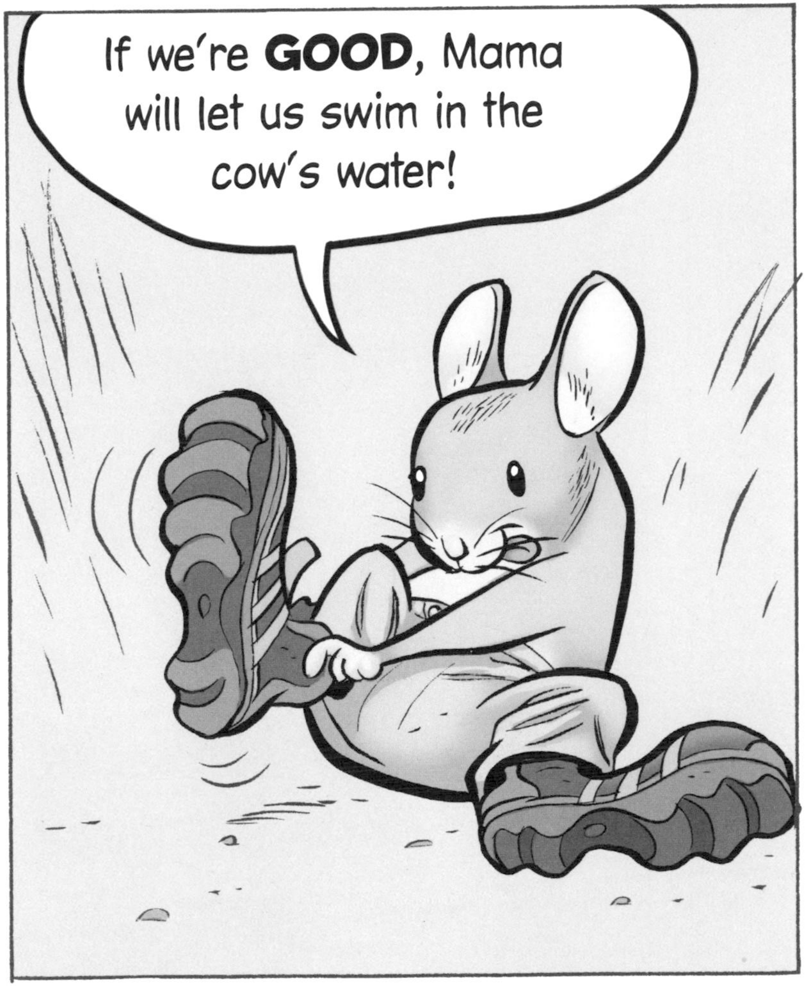
If we're **GOOD**, Mama will let us swim in the cow's water!

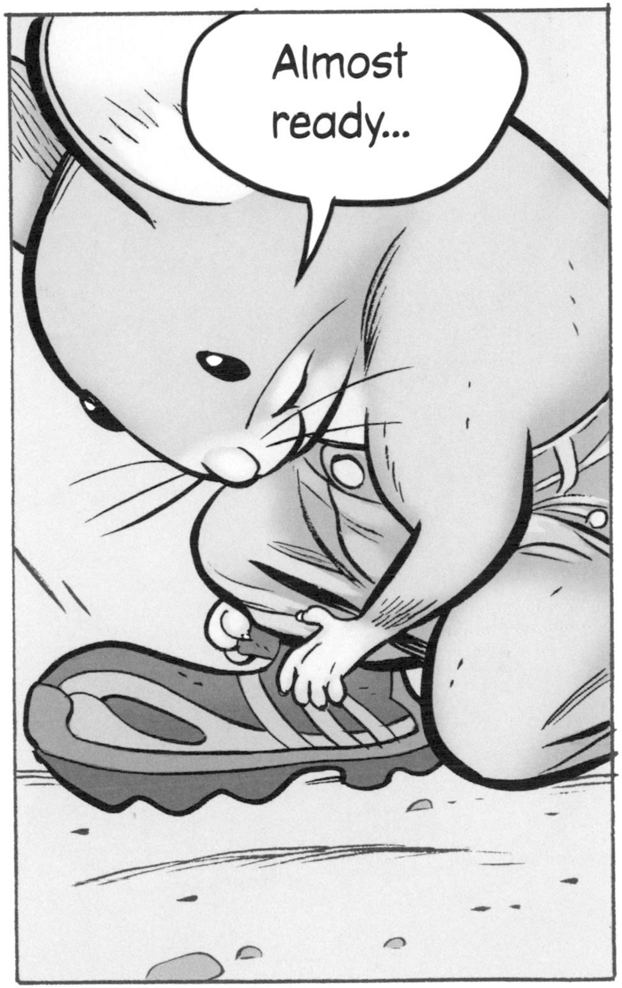
Almost ready...

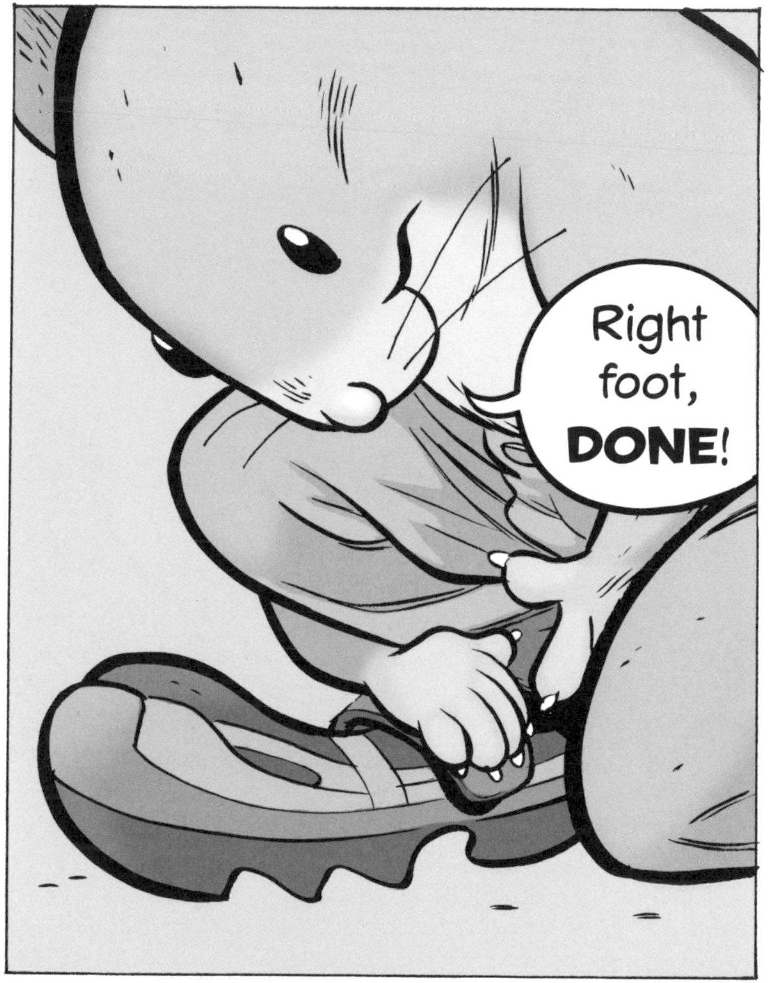
Right foot, DONE!

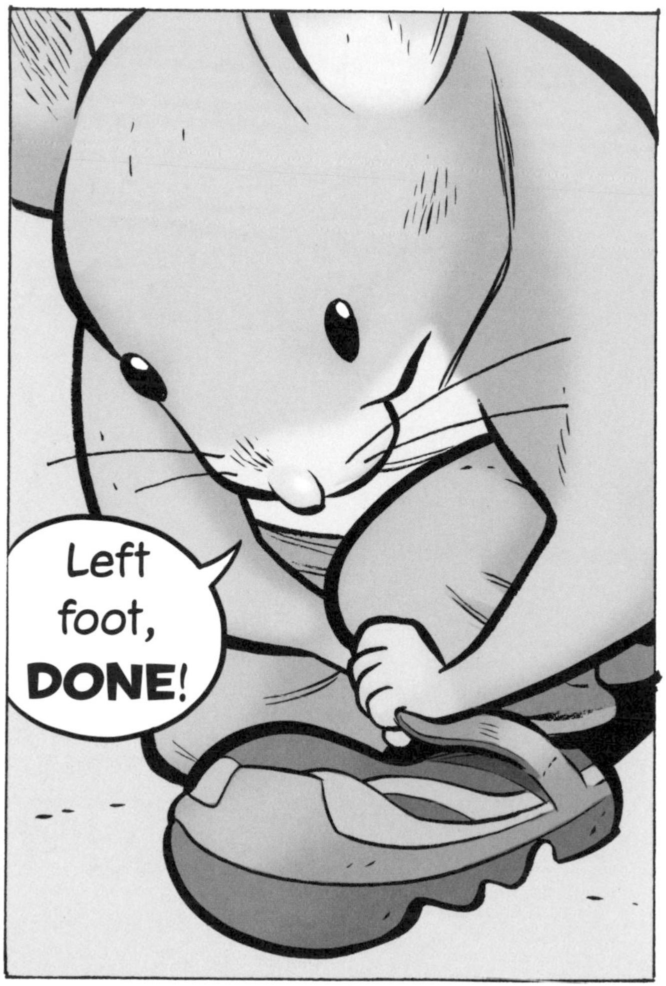
Left foot, DONE!

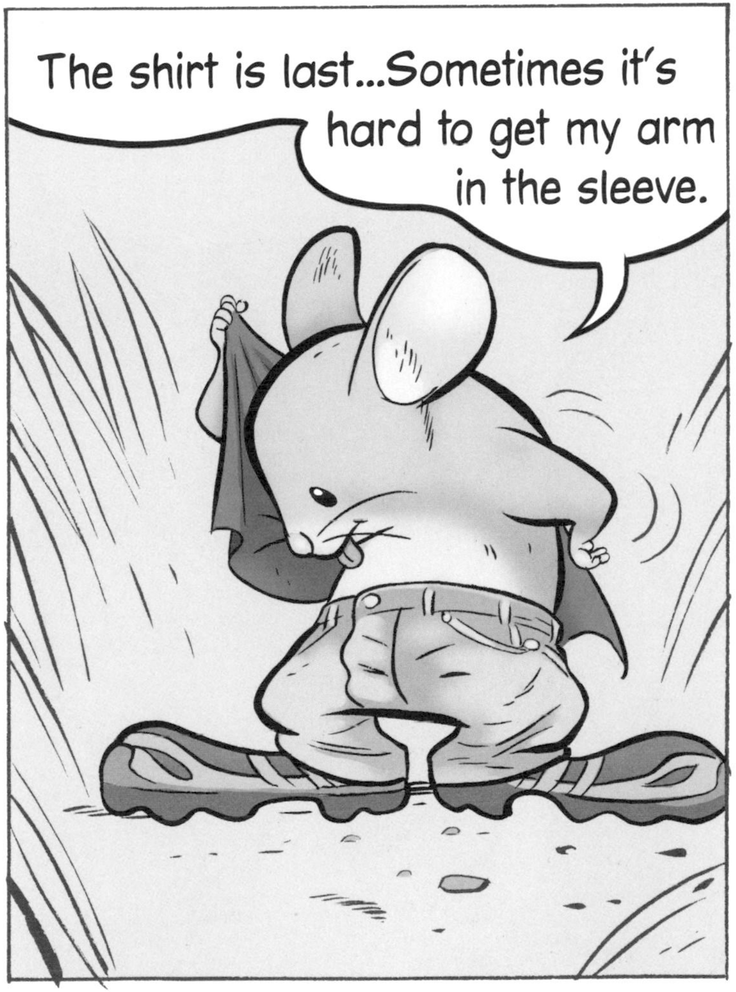
The shirt is last...Sometimes it's hard to get my arm in the sleeve.

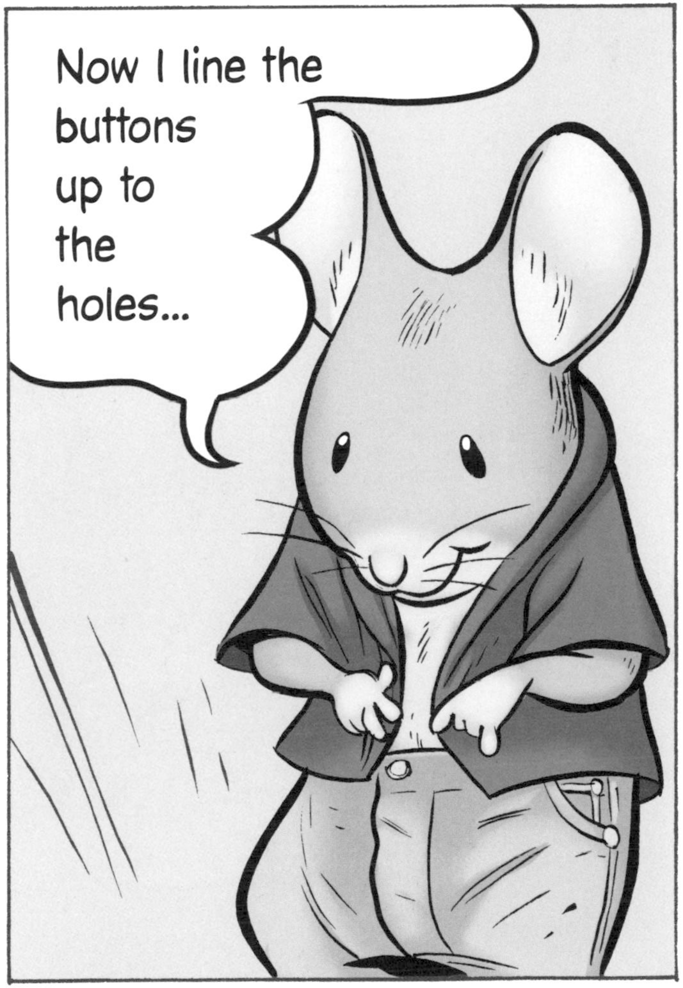
Now I line the buttons up to the holes...

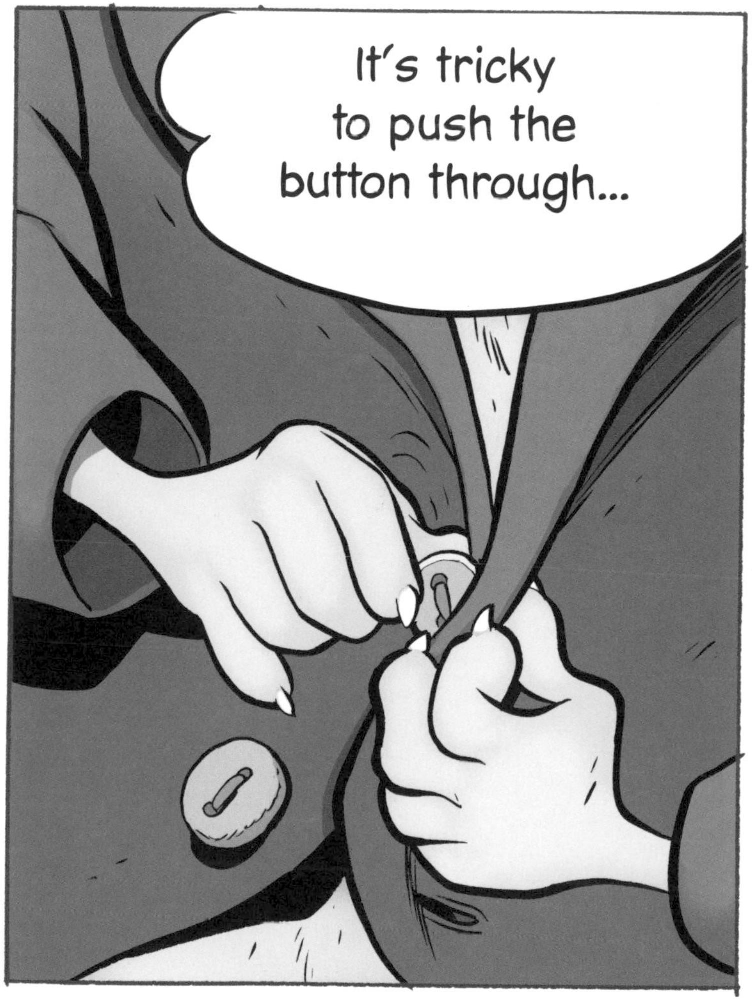
It's tricky to push the button through...

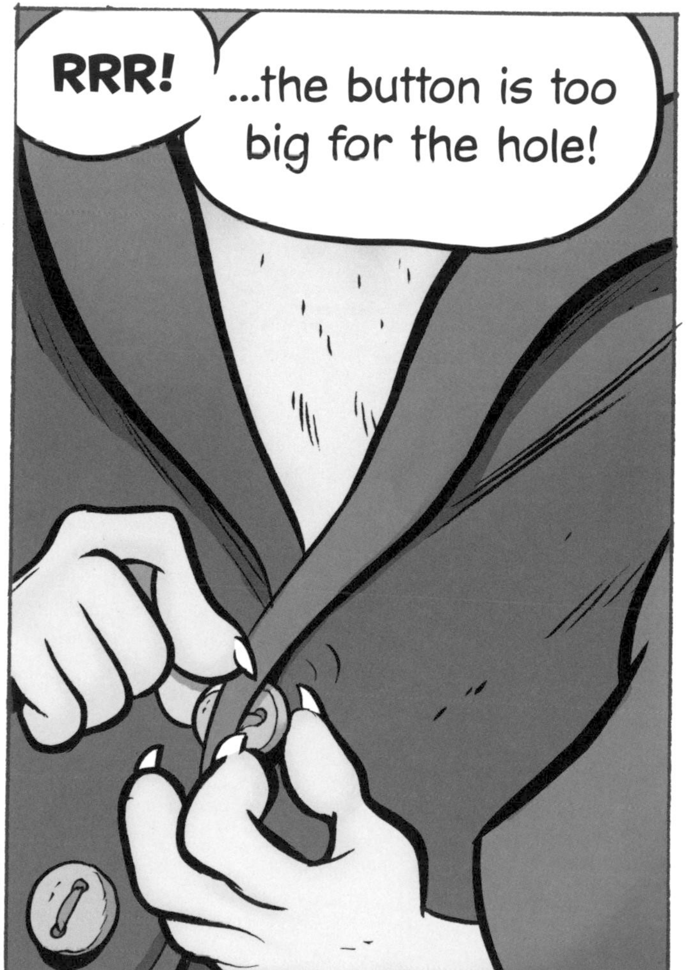
RRR!
...the button is too big for the hole!

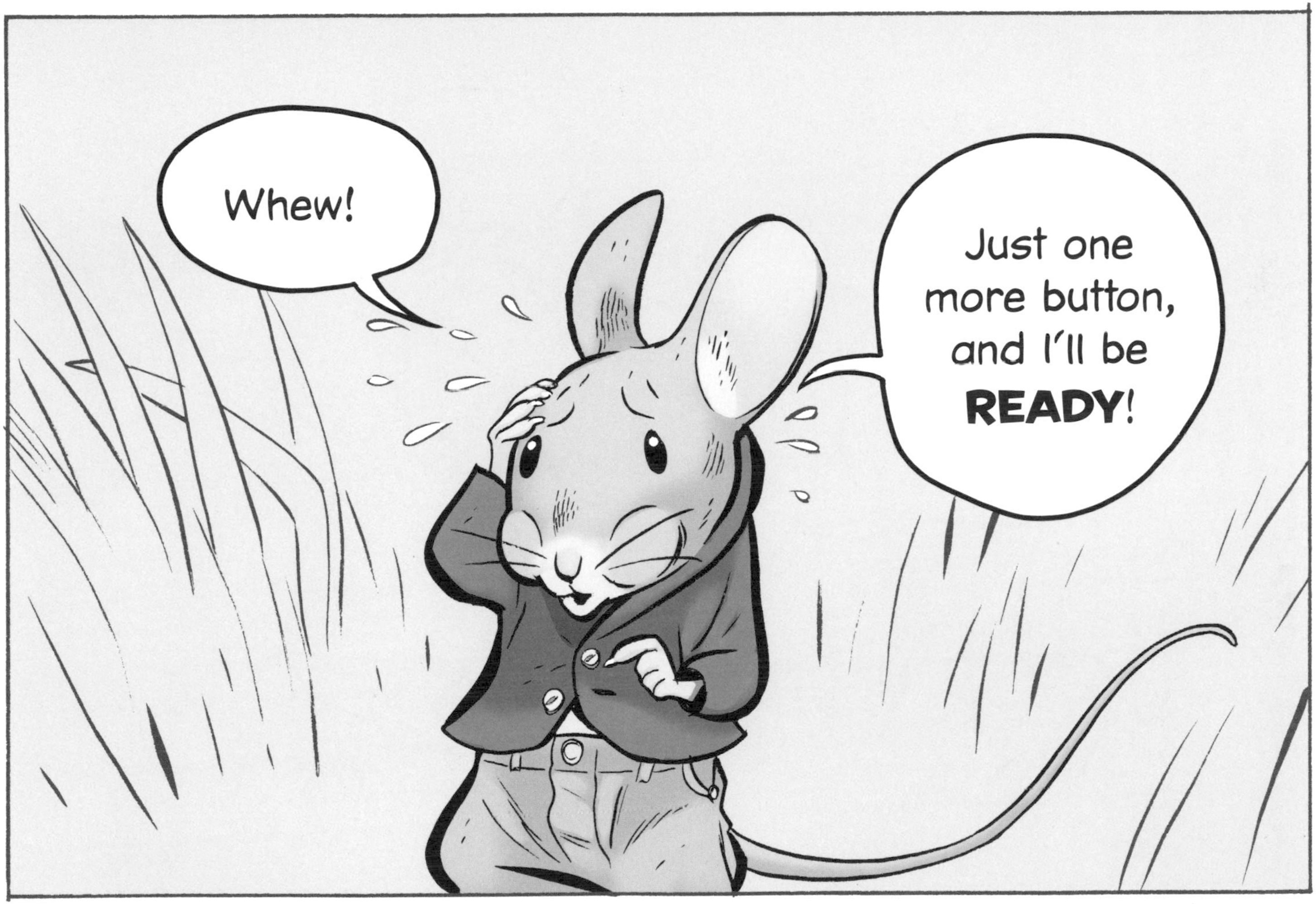
Whew!
Just one more button, and I'll be **READY**!

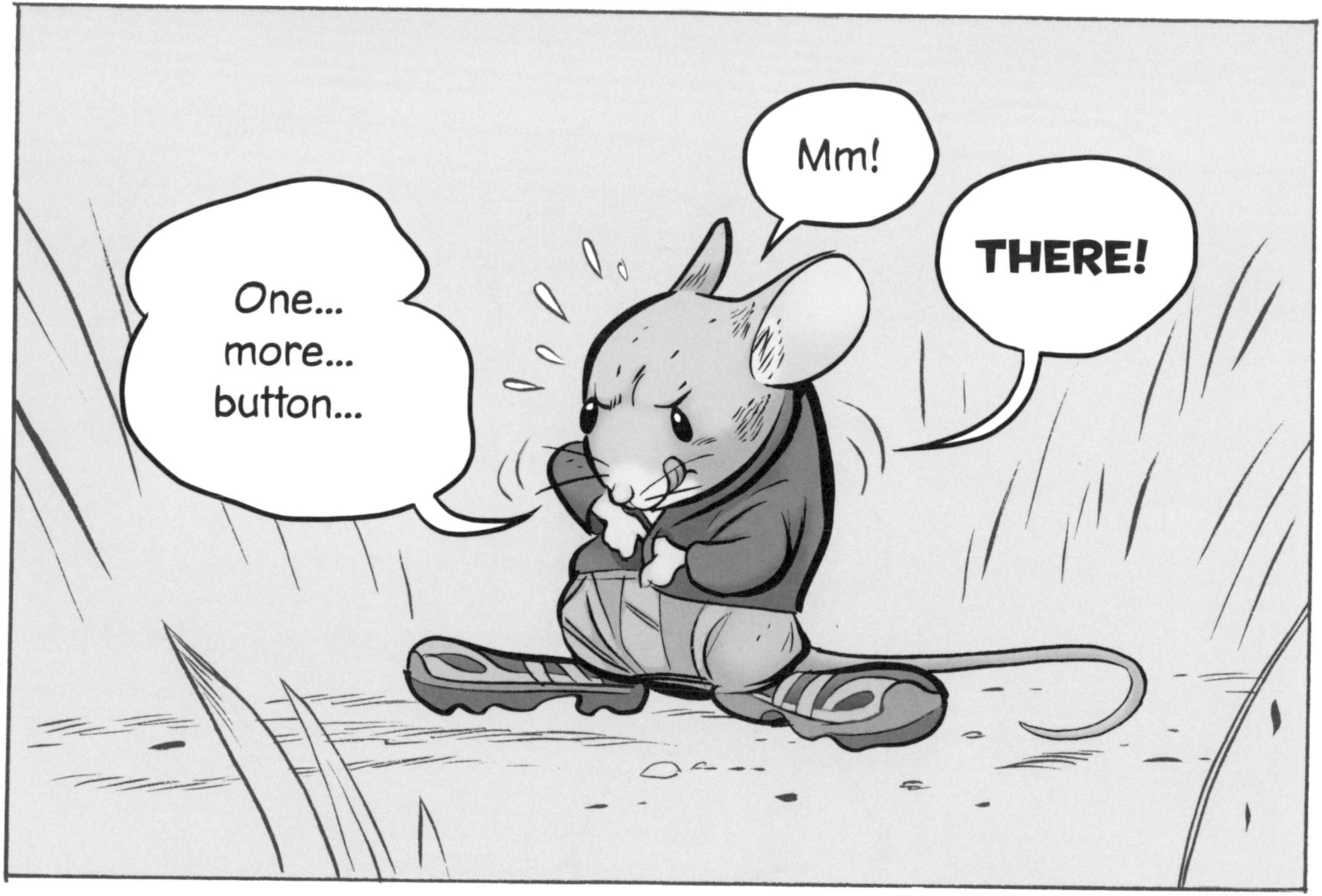
One... more... button...
Mm!
THERE!

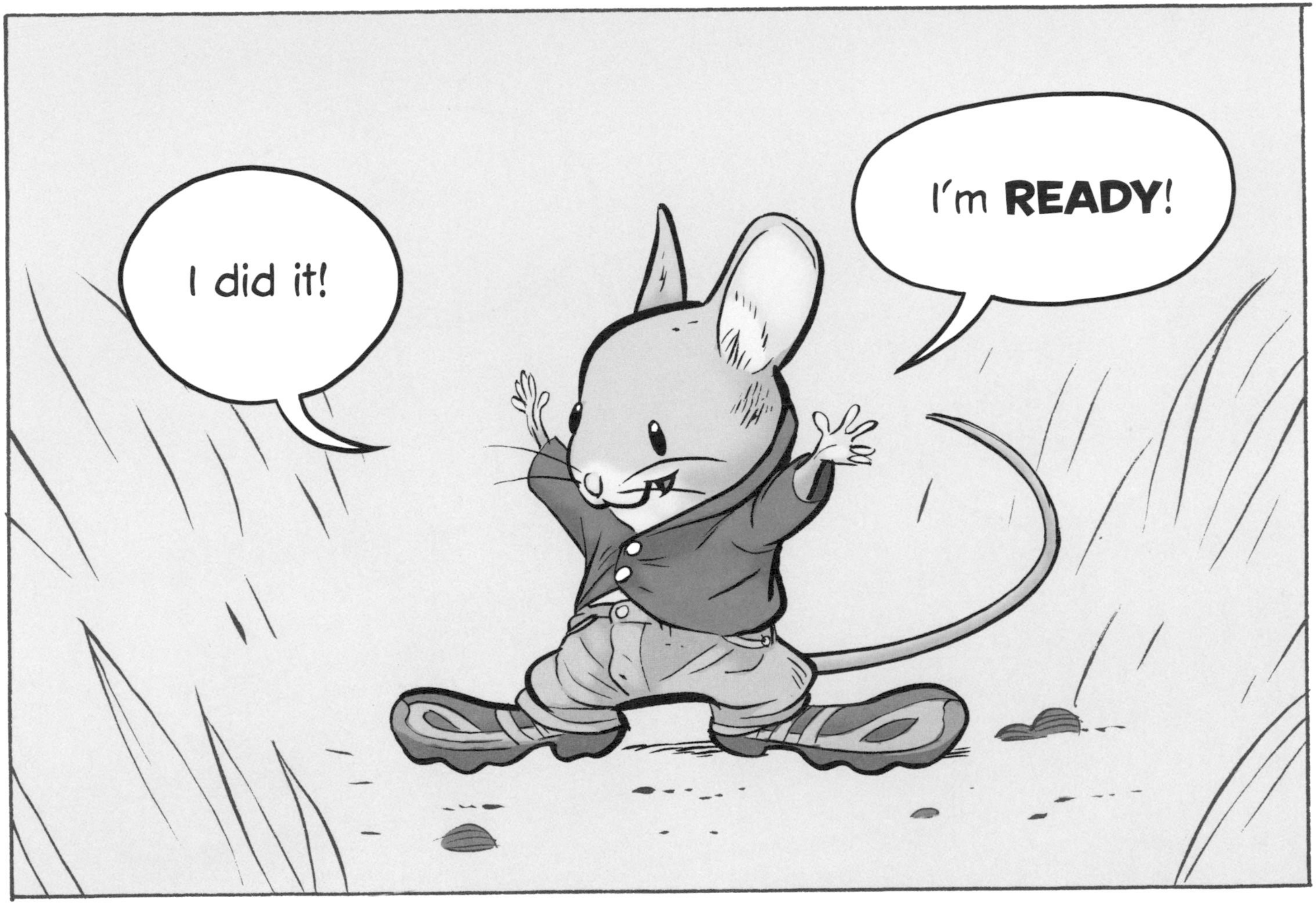
I did it!
I'm **READY**!

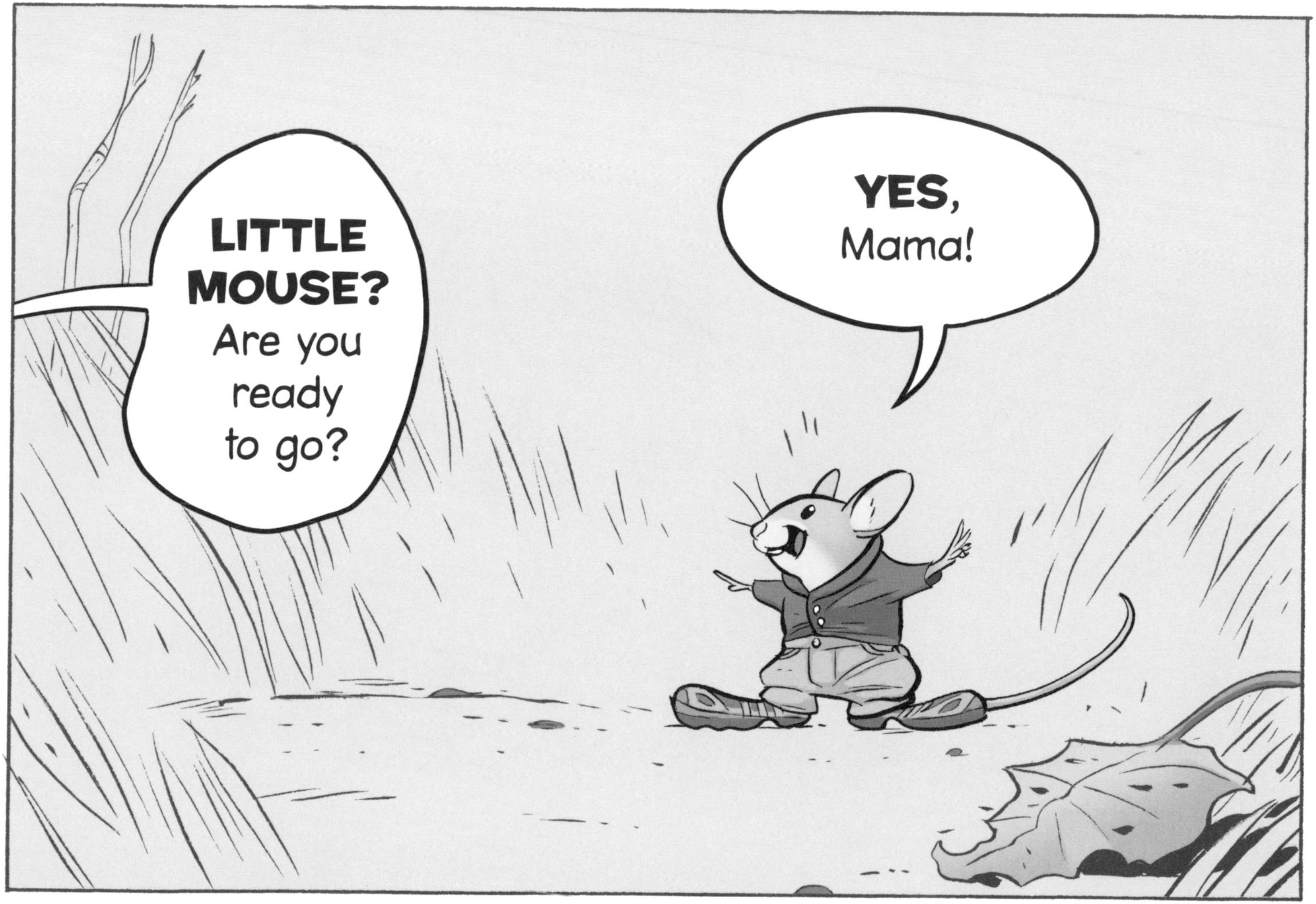
LITTLE MOUSE? Are you ready to go?
YES, Mama!

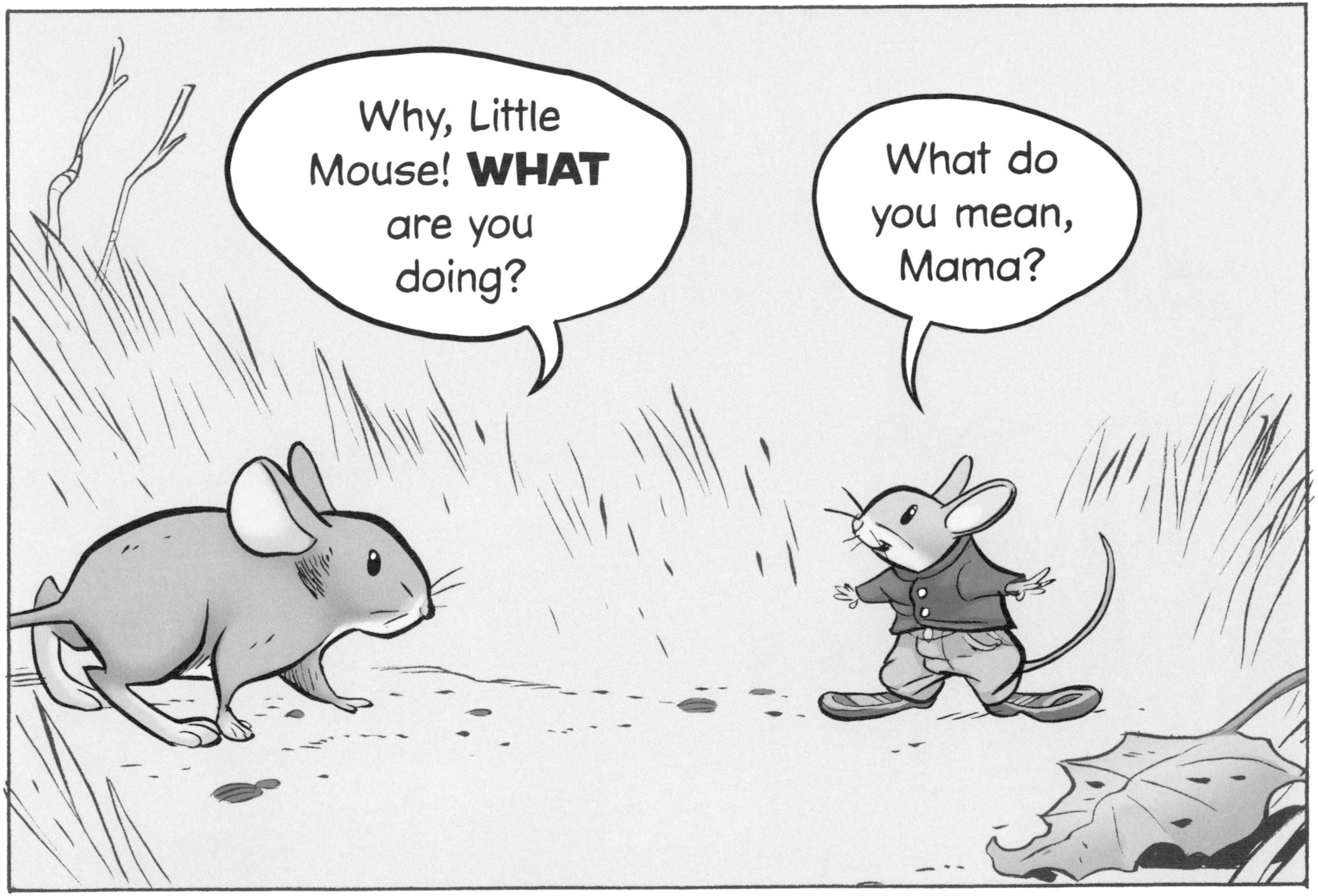
Why, Little Mouse! **WHAT** are you doing?
What do you mean, Mama?

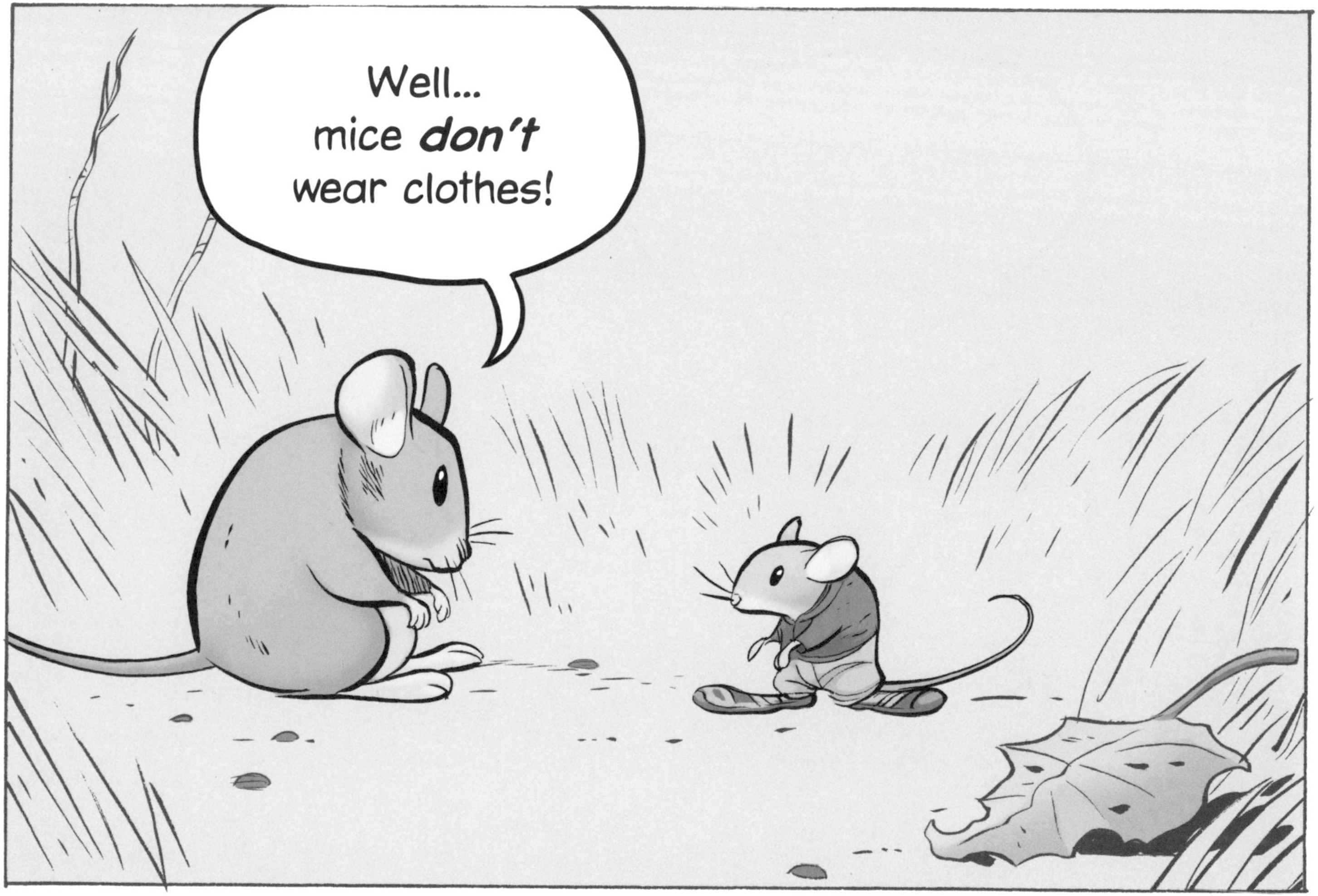
Well... mice ***don't*** wear clothes!

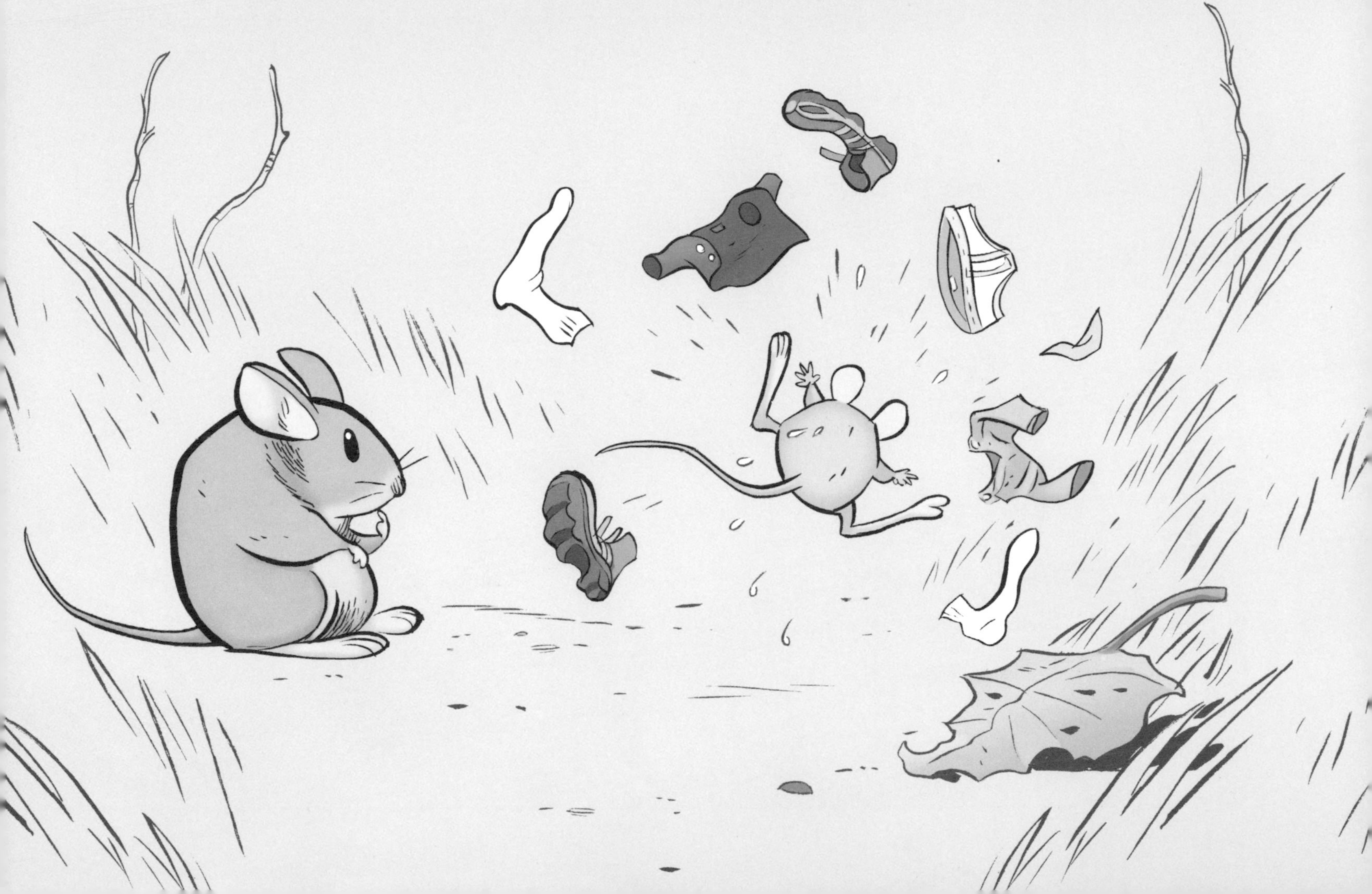

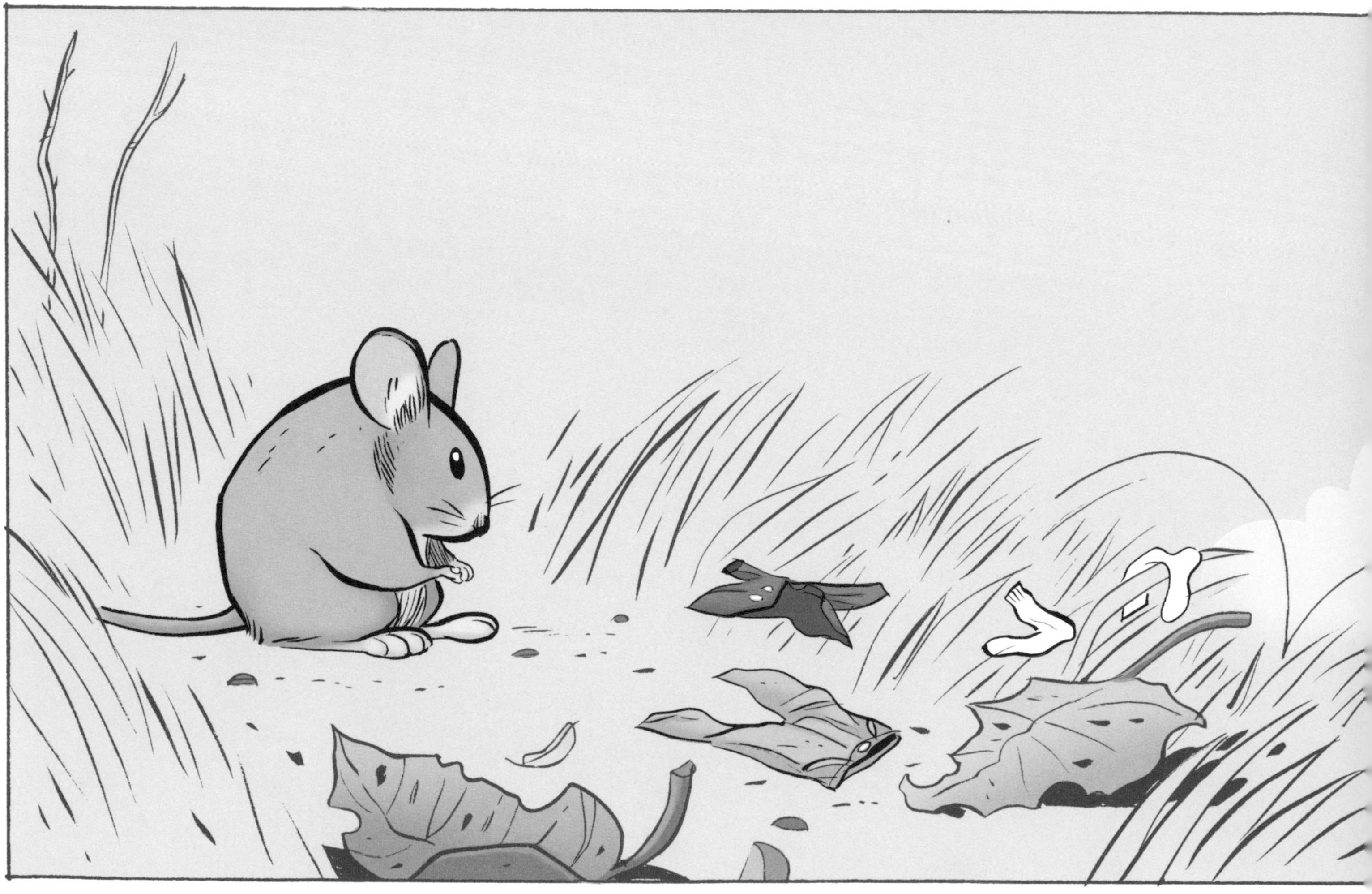

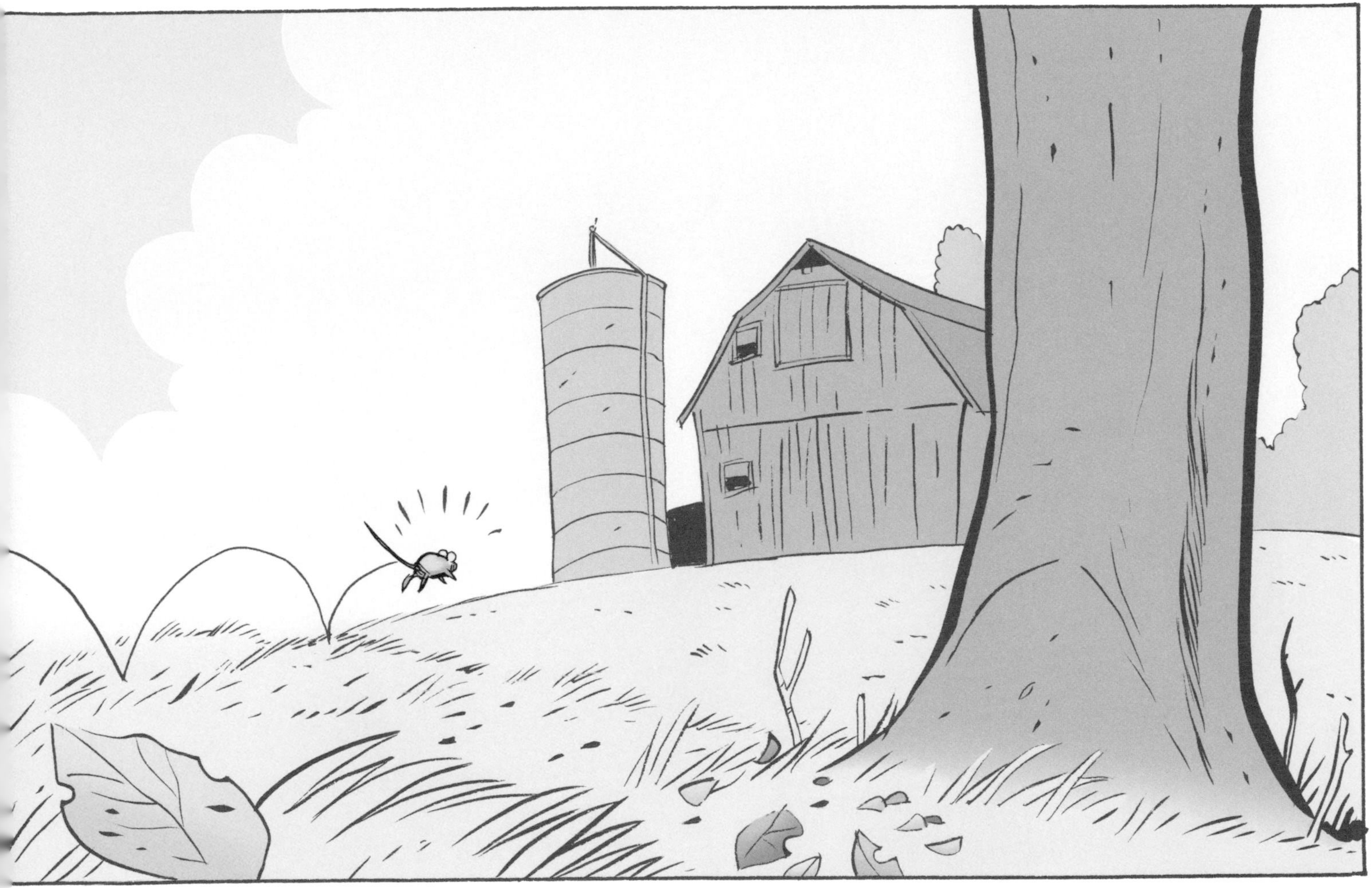

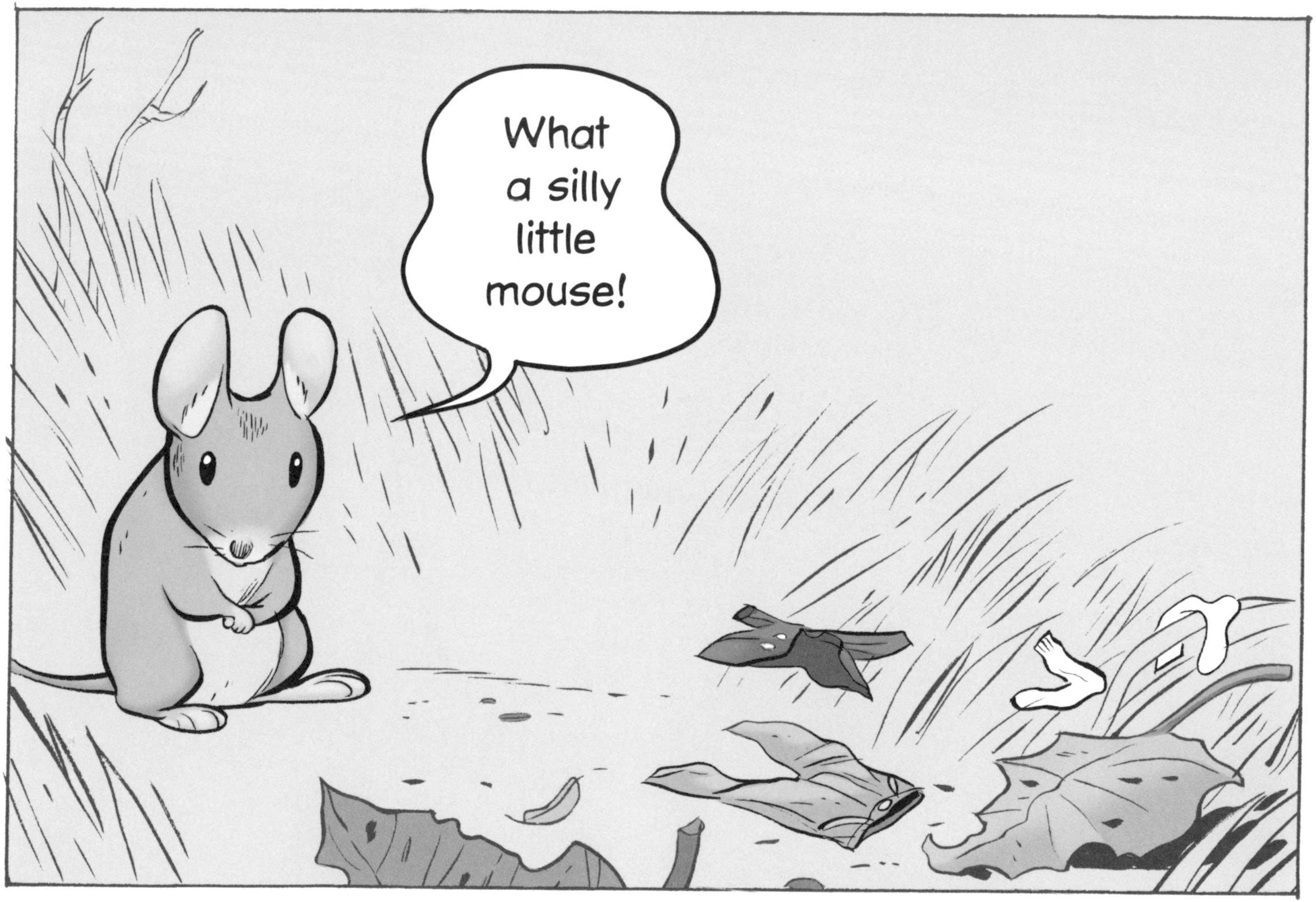
What a silly little mouse!

THE END

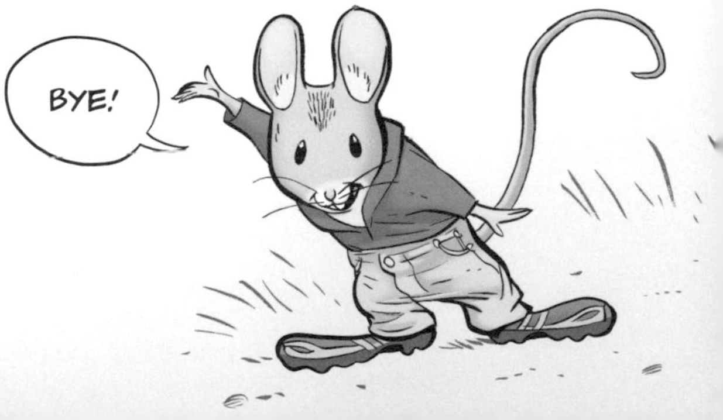
BYE!

ABOUT THE AUTHOR

When **JEFF SMITH** was growing up in a small town in Ohio, he loved cartooning, but he never imagined all the places comics would take him. With the help of his wife, Vijaya, Jeff created, published, and sold his comic book *BONE*. Jeff hadn't created *BONE* specifically for kids, but his fantastic tale of three cousins lost in a strange land appealed to all readers, including children, and it went on to sell millions of copies. *BONE* won multiple Eisner and Harvey Awards, and *TIME* called it one of the ten greatest graphic novels of all time. In 2008, Jeff's work was the subject of a major museum exhibit at the Wexner Center Galleries in Columbus, Ohio. His other books include *Shazam! The Monster Society of Evil* and *RASL*. This is his first book created just for young readers.